By: Cheraee C.

BROWN PAPER SUGA

MOCY PUBLISHING
WWW.MOCYPUBLISHING.COM

Detroit, Michigan

Brown Paper Suga

ISBN 978-1-940831-39-8

Published by Mocy Publishing, LLC.
Website: www.mocypublishing.com
Email: info@mocypublishing.com

ACKNOWLEDGEMENTS

I give special acknowledgments to all the amazing and talented writers who crafted and submitted works for this brilliant project. I hope to take this journey again with another novel dedicated to poetry and short stories.

LL Marie

Dominique Williams

Sunshine Sims

Pamela "PDot" Willis

J Focuz

Lawrence J.

TABLE OF CONTENTS

Excerpts from Cheraee C. Novels

Deviancy: I Love The Thrill

Liq-Trocity

Another Shady Mission

On Another Shady Mission

The Shadiest Mission Ever

BROWN PAPER SUGA

By: Cheraee C.

I'm dark skinned and he's darker

call the darkness brown, brown skin fine

a signature on a paperback book started it

its an underground love thang

that requires a postage stamp

and a sweet letterhead

the way he writes me

it's like his fingertips are elite

they entice me with delight

his pen strokes know how to provoke me

and get me open so I daydream every day

we take turns engulfing in a correctional confidential

ballpoint play

no fancy cursive sway

the brown-skinned riddles of notoriousness

keep me, seniority is submissive

filling me up like nutrients

slick verbs of enrichment

loving him, reading him, writing him is addictive

we got a lined paper commitment

whatever type of paper he can align

I can sip on the finest wine and unwind

between the thin lines and dinner

it might seem like a sweet fairytale but its pen winters

when nothing goes written and pen fights

raise blood pressures and fracture futures like wounds and

sutures

its bitterness in the sweetness and the waist deepness

pauses of friction and causes of briefness

the brown sugar and paper concoction

explains the history and the chemistry…

SQUARE ONE

By: Cheraee C.

I've returned to this domestic state

plain faced and vain placed

writing my rights and righting my wrongs

like oh my god, god you told me so

I felt the red signals, the red flags, the jet lag

my head hurts. my heart hurts, my feet hurt

all those footsteps, love songs, and sweet nothings

redirected me

direct me directly

the mending, the recovery

I'm sick of healing, retrying, rewinding, reviving, and

realigning

myself with that one thing

one love, one lover, one wish

my hips, my lips, and my gifts

tangled, strangled, my bangles

wrist me and risk me

diss me or frisk me

I'm in deep carelessness from no caresses

I feel so thumped and jumped

I was just on cloud nine

which cloud is mines?

which cloud is my mind?

how did I drift and shift so far behind?

all the blemishes I wore in my last new beginning

I didn't expect no happy endings or winnings

I don't know if it's all over

what I do know is I'm back at square one...

INSECURE LOVE

By: LL Marie

By this time I thought I would have had it figured out

I keep fucking with these insecure niggas who keep ripping my soul out

By this time I thought I would have found love or it found me

Surrender to what is, let go of what was, have faith in what will be

This is what I keep telling me, what's going to be will be

Maybe I should just sit back and wait on Mr. Right

But you can never find peace avoiding life

Shit fuck it maybe I should go out and be a slut and get fucked

After I think about it really none of these dudes worth my suck

Foolish girls react, wise ones talk

But I think you like that shit, cause you turned your back and walked

With no hidden agenda or negative thoughts

I really thought you were worth it, so I fought.

Now it's fuck me cause you got caught!!

My actions were louder than any words

And you came home and that fuckery still occurred

I did everything I could to prove I was on the team

I guess I was real foolish cause it was all a dream

I played Russian roulette with my heart and I lost as your see

Fuck it, I'm going to rebound and be on top once again like a G

All I can say is I fell for this dude and I don't know why

I put in major work and he still didn't try

I'm too damn sexy and beautiful to continue to cry

If you didn't see or appreciate my value

That's ok one day someone will tell ya!

But by that time it will be too late

My love I had would have turned into hate.

You had your rider and I chose to wait

You chose your actions and our fate

Never wish you bad wish you the best

One day you will realize what you had was better than the rest…

The Affiliation of Richard Moss

By: LL Marie

My name is Richard Moss and I'm currently being held as
a prisoner in the Michigan Department of Corrections. I've
been sentenced to serve seven to fifteen years for a crime I
didn't commit. I've been charged with a Controlled
Substance crime, in which my old lady overdosed from.
Since I've been incarcerated, I've done a lot of thinking.
Where is everyone who claims they love me? Where is my
mother of all people? My mind, body and soul are not
feeling this situation!

Does anyone give a damn that I'm locked up for a crime I
didn't commit? I'm living a nightmare and suffocating at
the same time. I need some money and no one has sent me
a dime! The only person who loves me without any strings
attached is my daughter, Mirah. Her love for me is
unconditional. My mother only loves me when she is

receiving something from me, although I gave up my childhood for her.

Everything, I've ever did in life was to help my mother. While growing up, we didn't have a damn thing. My mother couldn't hold it together, once my grandmother passed. At one point, we were sitting in the dark, because our lights and gas was turned off. The state was threatening to separate my family, so I stepped up to help my mother and four brothers. I couldn't allow anyone to separate us. Our neighborhood dope man needed a runner, so I applied for the job.

The streets needed a new soldier and I was young, black and hungry at the time and prison wasn't even an option at fourteen. I was enthusiastic and full of energy. I loved it and took pride in my shit and my employer was impressed. Getting that job, brought money into the house. Our lights and gas was never in threat of being turned off again. We ate good; my brothers and I were able to wear whatever was hot. No more hand me downs or Salvation Army clothing. My moms' was also able to buy some of the things she liked. That was a big jump from almost being in the system to having options.

I worked as a runner for years and eventually got my brothers on board as well. Ronnie and Tee couldn't hang, but Sway was a perfect fit. I grew up hustling and my mother supported the game. How could she not? We were raised around dope men. My uncles, granddaddy was all dope men. As the years rolled by, my brother Sway got as good as me hustling; maybe better. He and I started doing it big. The hood knew who we were. We were neighborhood stars. I had plenty of money and plenty friends, so I thought.

Once I got old enough and save enough money I moved from Cent's crib. I never looked back! I wore the finest of suits, drove dopest cars, pockets stayed fat and kept a bad broad on my arm. I could get my freak on any time I wanted. It was nothing for me to sleep with two to three women at a time, while my woman watched. I was living the American dream, shit I was probably living my daddy's dream too, if I knew that mutherfucka. I lived the life that most strive for. I've eaten at the finest restaurants and partied with the best. I got high on some of the finest China, greenest green and on an assortment of pills that looked like Skittles.

My brother Sway and I were tight as hell. We were inseparable when we were young. I taught him everything I know. We were an unbreakable force back then. I had a good relationship with all my brothers, but Sway was my shot. We owned those streets. Right now, Sway is the King on the streets. Now, I question my relationship with all my brothers, including Sway.

My mother eventually quit her job, because me and Sway had her back. We cashed her out daily. She bought herself a Jag, jewelry, clothing, expensive liquor and furnisher for her house. We made sure she didn't want for nothing. Even tho, she eventually got a man, she still depended on us to take care of her spoiled ass.

I never had a chance to enjoy my childhood after my grandma died. I gave it all up to help Cent and my brothers! That's because Cent was young, and just as immature as me and my brothers. That was exactly why my grandma got all the respect and was called ma. Cent is more like a sister, or friend than a mother. She's selfish as hell and will always be. Let's just be real, Cent only cares about how we can benefit her and make her life comfortable.

Cent was 'Ms. Party Over here', always trying to keep up appearances. I could see in her eyes that she really wanted a simple life, but she didn't know how to obtain it. As her son, I wanted that for her too. Thinking back, I didn't want our family living in stress and strife, but I didn't know how to obtain it the right way. But in my head I continued to think "Why should we live in poverty, when we didn't have to?" So I put that work in and my entire family benefitted from the dope game. When I decided to make that commitment, we all enjoyed the lavish toys, and carefree lifestyles, with cocky altered egos to match. My family reaped the benefits of drug money and lived a decent existence, because of me. I stood up for them, I sacrificed myself for them.

My only regret is that I didn't invest in myself. I was too busy chasing fast money and women. I was living what I thought was the 'good life.' I had a ball and enjoyed the hell out of my life. I wish I would have had more to show for my sacrifice, I was too busy playing 'Big Papa.' I wanted to be like my uncles and ballers in the streets, never thinking of the consequences. I wanted my name to mean something in those streets. My wanted my mother to be praised and my brothers to be feared.

Now, as a man, I sit in this prison cell as a fixture. I live a life void of any feelings, no money, no dreams, no glory, no more ambition and no friends. I put a whole lot of money in people pockets and where are they now? I'm reduced to a piece of flesh breathing with a number. My soul hurts, because I feel used and never prepared myself for this chapter of my life. The person who I was, I am not any longer. I'm afraid of who I have become or will be. I'm almost ashamed of myself. I do know I'm angry and feel alone, but that doesn't mean shit to anyone.

The person, who I loved the most, gave up the most for, won't even help me. How could she be so cruel? She deposed of me, like I wasn't shit. She won't even put money on her phone, so that I can call her or money in my account so I can eat. She doesn't care if I survive or not. She acting like I'm dead weight and drowning her. She doesn't even encourage my brothers to reach out to me. I actually need my momma and she acts as if she only has four sons.

DESPITE IT ALL, I STILL LOVE HER! That's my momma, that's my Cent. I ask myself, would I do it again?

Probably yes, but a little different. I wouldn't allow Cent to get totally off the hook of being a mother. My grandmother carried Cent, and then Sway and I carried her. She has never been forced to support us or anyone. If I had to do over, I would make her carry half the burden of helping our family, instead of me acting as if I was her husband. I took on a burden that it wasn't my job, trying to save my family. I just grew up too fast and was in a hurry to be a man. I screwed myself and now I'm paying for it.

I don't proclaim to innocent on how I played my role in life, but I'm innocent of being responsible for Sheila overdosing. She had been getting high for years. She was so bad off into those drugs; she had to main line, just to get the full effects of the dope. She freely decided to get high and she did. Why, the state wanted to make me responsible for her death; I don't know. Yeah, I gave her the drugs, but so what! Sheila would get dope from anyone she could.

Now, I've been charged and convicted of giving Sheila the drugs that killed her. This case sounds like a victimless crime to me. I'm in prison, because she overdosed. How stupid does that sound?

I went from being the man to being reduced to an juvenile. I don't get to make decisions for myself. I'm told what to do, my every step. My individuality has ceased. I'm in a place where love isn't kind, but is taken for weakness. In this place, there are records of my wrongs, egos are inflated and pride seems to prevail. There's plenty of envy, along with bragging and boasting every day. In this place everyone seems self-seeking, arrogant and rude. This place is empty of any kind of love and kindness; which means, I'm in a living hell! Each day feels like I'm living in a coffin. I'm dead on the inside. I really want to die, but lack the nerve to do something about it.

I keep getting these crazy and dumb tattoos, just to feel the pain. I feel something when that needle burns into my flesh. Otherwise, I would be cutting on myself, just to feel something; anything. I put on a strong front for everyone to see. I can't allow anyone to see that I'm really scared and feel alone. If only someone in my family would reach out to me and make me feel like I belong, than this being in here would be somewhat bearable.

I have to keep myself uplifted daily. I try to remind myself that my body is in prison, not my mind. Hopefully, I can keep my mind focus on the positive. If I can't than I will perish in here. Sometimes I want to give up and surrendered my mind, body and soul to the madness in here. I don't want this to be my norm. I refuse to get comfortable in here.

I don't want a television, no gym shoes, no sunglasses; nothing. I just want out! I want a little buzz every now and then, but nothing else. I don't ever what to feel good in here. Once I get comfortable, that means I have accepted my fate and that I've succumbed. As far as relationship with anyone in the joint, what is that? Cats in here get the wrong message about friendships and relationships. I don't want any wrong wires crossed. I have associations; people I'm cool with, but no friends.

Who can I really trust? I wish I could have had a real relationship with Cent or one of my brothers. It's obvious, if I'm not giving something to someone than I have no one. Everyone in my world is a receiver, especially my mother. Right now, I just exist. I don't even know if God knows I'm here. I'm going to make it, because I've always been bullet proof. I always have been and always will be! I'm made to survive; I keep telling myself. Maybe Cent will get a conscience and remember she has a son locked away; maybe. I'm Richard Moss and this is my tale of my affiliations and afflictions! Don't worry about me, because I'm a survivor. I'm going to make it; really!

MR. SCOTT

By: Dominique Williams

As an adult you wanna believe that you have everything figured out. But as a woman? We think everything is a sign, especially when it comes to love like me for example. My name is Vivian and I've been on and off with someone I've loved since I was 17, but now I'm 26. Sure we took a break for a long in between time, but he made his way back. So we're supposed to be together....right? 'RIGHT?!... I shouted that to myself in the mirror this morning as I was brushing my teeth and washed my face. This morning was a dreadful one. My best friend of eight years was going to prison and it was the hardest thing to witness or even comprehend. I was wiping my tears away and telling myself to be a big girl and to be strong for my friend. Taelor was a good girl, she didn't do nothing to nobody. She was just in a bad situation, she needed money. Hell we all did, but Taelor wanted it fast and NOW! That's why we're in this position now, she was willing to get cash anyway she can, soft porn, stealing from people...you name is she did it. As a best friend who only wanted the best for her I could only tell her so much. Everyone looked at me with the side eye when she was arrested, they assumed I knew something about it or that I didn't care enough to stop her...but I did. This goes back to us adults thinkin that we have it all figured out because she didn't listen to a word I said. There was a loud horn outside interrupting my thoughts, I looked outside and it was Brock. The guy I've had puppy love for since I was a kid. He had always been there, we've never made anything official, we've never even had sex but our love was beyond physical. We're adults now, I can't ruin my mind with fairytales and what ifs.

"Coming!!" I yelled out the window for his reassurance.

Brock and I haven't hung out in years at this point, but we shared a mutual friend, Taelor. Even though she was my friend, he knew her through me and always kept in touch with her. Even when I moved on and had another man in my life he was still around, asking about me and my well being. She was like the glue that stuck us together. So today we were going to give a short goodbye to our friend for a few years.

"This is crazy," he said as I finally got in the car.

"I know right?! I can't believe that she's going away...." I said as I looked down trying to hold back the tears.

"Naw I'm not talking about that, I'm talking about how years later it STILL takes you forever just to get ready." He said with a laugh, trying to lighten the mood. I cracked a smirk. Nothing could get my head off of my friend. We walked into the court room, everyone was already seated. Friends and family filled the room waiting

27

to see my friend off. As the judge said her final words and my friend looked back at me one last time it seemed the whole room went dark and a howl of crying came over me. As the months went by, I grew stronger realizing that my friend wasn't here but we always wrote each other and I was a regular visiting her in prison. Our phone calls were always the best!

" Hello?? I said as the line was finally clear of the operator directing our call.

"Yea," she said to confirm everything.

"How are you? I miss you," I spoke as though we didn't see each other a few days ago.

"Girl I just saw you, relax!" She laughed.

"Whatever, so what's been up? You got any good letters.." I said in reference to her scumbag ex-boyfriend.

"Naw not really, only person that's been writing me outside of family and friends is Brock.." I rolled my eyes to the back of my head. Brock and I haven't talked since a few days after Taelor's sentencing. He was a liar, always has been and Taelor knew it too.

"Well whatever, how about the people in there? They treating you okay?" Trying to change the subject I wanted to know about her prison life.

"Don't whatever him! You know I think Brock is perfect for you, he's the one for you," she said in reference to me changing the subject.

"But life in here is the same old same old. I've made 2 new friends but ain't no friends in here. Everybody for themselves." I ended the conversation with my friend as it went on for another 30 minutes. I thought about all the things she said, even the ones I didn't wanna hear. The next few days went by slow, no calls from my friend. Browsing through Facebook I noticed a message, it was from Brock. He was in my inbox like always, checking up on me. Also, informing me about the new things going on in his life, like his new girlfriend and the apartment they share.

"Yea I love her, I think we stay in the apartments you used to stay in a while ago." I stared at his reply, debating if I wanted to respond even though I didn't care for anything he said. Instead I wished him the best with his relationship, that I loved him and to keep in touch. He ended the convo with an ' I love you more' but I didn't respond.

"Vivian why is he always writing you telling you about his life like you give a damn?" My friend Draya said as I caught her up on the latest Brock update.

"I don't know, maybe it's his way of keeping contact and tabs on me," I said with a laugh. Just like that, my phone started to light up with message after message.

"Dang who is that?" Draya said with wide eyes as she too saw my phone light up continuously as if there was an emergency. I looked down at my phone and was instantly pissed. These messages were from an anonymous number, and from the looks of things it was a girl. She was very adamant about me talking to her boyfriend and to stay away from him. She called me all type of whores, she even said I had an STD! All of these messages confused me, what was this girl talking about? And most of all, WHO WAS SHE? This mysterious woman knew very few things about me, majority of it were lies. After respectfully asking who she was, she only continued to bark and told me her identity was irrelevant and to stay away from her man. The man she never mentioned or hinted at, I was so confused. Who was she talking about? Don't get me wrong, I'm no angel. I may have gave some of my attention to a guy with a girlfriend, but we didn't sleep together. For the past few days Draya and I tried our hardest to find out who this person could be. I've hit up every guy in my phone to ask about girlfriends I did and didn't know about, and of course no one had a clue who I was talking about.

"Well maybe it's Brock's girlfriend! That's the only one that makes sense," Draya said in a tone that sounded like she was giving up on this quest.

"But it can't be! Brock doesn't have my number, we only communicate on Facebook. How would she get my number?.." I replied just as tired as she. We both her and I sat in silence trying to piece everything together. The next day I fought back the resistance to inbox Brock, so instead I called him on Facebook.

"Hey," I started off. He smiled in the camera and it seemed to ripple from there. I told him about the unpleasant messages and the obvious connection to him.

"Sorry wrong guy playa," he said with a chuckle. That instantly made me mad.

"Why are you laughing?! Get cho bitch!!" I said out of anger.

"Whoa calm down, it couldn't be her," he said with a weary look on his face due to my hefty response.

"And why can't it be Brock!?!" I was very frustrated by this time.

"Because I don't have your number Vivian. How would she be able to text you?.." He was right, how would she be able to? Touché. I thought to myself, but I didn't let him know. I just simply hung up in his face. This was a waste of time; I'll never find out who that whore is. Brock called me on Facebook days after that, continuously both writing and trying to video chat me, but I never responded. He didn't want anything, I thought to myself. Weeks had gone by before I saw a message from Brock that made me stop in my tracks.

"What if we're supposed to be together?" I called him on Facebook after that.

"What are you talking about?" I said with a straight faced and an annoyed tone.

"You know how I feel about you, I love you. I never stopped..." I never did neither, but I couldn't tell him that. Plus what about his girlfriend? Didn't he live with her? Ain't she's the bitch that was playing on my phone? But I kept those comments to myself. He continued..

"I just wanna know if I'm with the right person. The girl I'm with now is forcing me into marriage and kids. It's not that I don't want to, but I don't want to make those type of decisions knowing that I still love you the way that I do." And just like that Brock and I were spending time together, a lot. Movies, dinner, I even snuck him in my room like old times. But as this week went by, I started to feel guilty. Even though Brock and I had chemistry and history, it didn't feel right trying to restore and work on this connection knowing that he had a girlfriend that he went home to every night. So to avoid confrontation, on our last date I stopped responding to his messages. It was a coward thing of me to do I know, but if I told him how I felt it'd only make things bad. Brock only got worse, he texted me all the time about his feelings and emotions. About how he felt toyed with and felt as though I only hit him up to go out on dates with him when I was bored.

"Viv, you've got to say something to him. Don't leave him in the dark," Draya said to me as I talked to her on the phone a few days after continually ignoring Brock's existence. Fine, I thought to myself so I texted him after hanging up with Draya. Brock was mad at me for ignoring him, but he wanted to see me in person. He was serious about it, and wouldn't take no for an answer until I at least met with him, so I let him come over. I came outside to meet him in his car with my jacket on. I got in the car silently, not making eye contact.

"What Brock?" My response was dry. He smiled, he pulled me in for a hug and began to kiss me. I pushed him off of me.

"Don't be like that Vivian, I missed you. Why you been ignoring me? You don't like me anymore? Am I somebody you talk to cause you bored?" I looked up at Brock as he was talking and I saw worry in his eyes. I could tell he was all the way in.

"No Brock it's not that, we just can't talk anymore," I shook my head in my reply. His face asked me a question before they could come out of his mouth, and before anything did come out of his mouth I replied

"You have a girlfriend! That you live with!! How am I supposed to be with someone and try and build when you have a whole female you live with?! How is that supposed to make me feel?!' I said in frustration with myself. How could I let someone allow me to get so emotionally involved so quick just because we had history as kids? We continued to go back and forth, He was adamant about me seeing things his way and understanding his undying love for me.

"OKAY!!!!" he shouted back at me.

"I'll leave her!!..." And he did, before you know it, within a week Brock was living back with his mom. He'd move all of his things out of the house he'd once shared with his now ex girlfriend. It was almost a shock, but for whatever reason I assumed that this was real. Brock must have really wanted this if he's willing to do all this just to be with me. Although we didn't make things official just yet, it felt like it. I couldn't believe that the guy I had puppy love for after all these years was actually the guy I called mine. He loved me right? He stopped everything with another woman because you he couldn't pretend and go on with a future with someone when all he ever wanted was to be with me. Two weeks went by and I'd never felt so good about something! We'd made it official, FINALLY. Taelor was beyond happy when I went to the prison for a visit to tell her the news in person.

' Yessss! I knew it, I'm so happy for y'all," she said with more excitement than me. Everything just seemed so perfect. Almost. That following morning I had three missed calls from Brock, we'd finally exchanged numbers. But before I could call him back I read his text messages, they read: 'I tried to stop her from writing you.' I knew who he was talking about already, so I went on Facebook and low and behold I'd had a message from his ex-girlfriend. Typical, I thought. Just another bitter ex. Her long letter started off with the random text messages I was getting from an anonymous number and how they weren't from her, which was weird. I didn't understand why she felt the need to explain herself. She then starts to ask if Brock and I were thinking about being together. Who did she think she was to write me questioning me? Brock didn't tell her?

Before I could answer she hit me with a bomb: 'I'm

pregnant.' I swear I stopped breathing for five minutes. I

stopped replying and instantly called Brock.

"Brock what is she talking about?!" I said the

second he answered his phone.

"She's been saying she's pregnant but she says that

ALL the time. "

"Well how do you know she's not lying about it

now?! You slept with her?!" I said in a hostile tone.

"Because I know she's not, and yes...." His voice

sounded guilty. I let out a scream, men are so stupid.

"But that was a few weeks ago! When you were

ignoring me and not answering my phone calls. I felt

lonely, I thought you didn't want me so...I had sex with her

cause I wanted to feel loved, but it was protected! And after

we were done I told her that we couldn't do it again because

of my feelings for you. She knows how I feel about you

Vivian. Everyone does, it's no secret how much I love you." I didn't know what he wanted me to do, but I can't talk to him. I don't talk or even give men the time of day with kids, I don't have any. Why should I?

"I'm sorry Brock...I can't ..."

He interrupted me, "don't say that! She's always saying that she's pregnant every since we've been together. She's just mad cause of how I left. She's trying to get me back babe, you have to believe me.

I sighed, "idk." Brock started begging and pleading. Until eventually I agreed to stick around until we found out the results. If she really was, then we'll take it from there. So until then Brock spoiled me. He bought me gifts, made time for me, made sure he woke up to me every day and told me how much he loved me and how happy he was to have me back in his life. I was happy, for the first time in a long time. In the back of my mind I was waiting for those results and I was anxious. Sunday football was on and Brock was glued to the TV. He loved football and even played fantasy football. As he screamed in excitement for his team his phone went off on the table. He looked at me as I looked at him, he'd made his way to the phone. He looked down at his messages and then up at me. The look in his face said it all. I looked down, trying to hold back the tears. I was so mad, mad at myself mostly.

"She's pregnant ain't she?..." He nodded. I was speechless. I tried to leave to get my thoughts together, to be mad at myself in peace, to cry my heart out behind closed doors, but Brock wouldn't let me. He didn't wanna be alone, and I didn't neither so I cried in his arms.

"I love you Vivian so much, I don't wanna lose you. I finally got you. I wish it was you! I wish you were the one that was pregnant. I've always wanted you to have my kids." I looked at him and saw the sincerity behind his eyes. Did he really mean it?

The next few months were a tough one. Brock had only argued with the now new mother of his child. She was super upset with him leaving her for me and how he did it. She'd changed her number and only contacted him by calling him on private numbers or emails. She also began to take it out on me. She constantly wrote me on Facebook and was able to find me on other social media to stalk me. It was becoming unbearable and I was sick of being the mature one. Brock wasn't being a man and stepping up, he was confused himself and very scared to possible lose out on a relationship with his daughter. He'd found out what he was having when his baby momma decided to call him private one day. After her and I were bickering back and forth it caused a real strain on my relationship with Brock. His bitter baby momma made it known that if he was to ever be with me after she gave birth that he would never see his child! This made Brock restless, sleepless, and even more confused. It was hard to see him hurting and I could do nothing about it. But what was I supposed to do? He asked for all of this not me. Things got so hard with Brock and I, we broke up all the time just to get back together. It was a rollercoaster. But the last time was the worst. So many things had been done by this point. Family was involved, everyone had already placed their opinions on me based off mf Brock's decision to come crying to me all because he wasn't happy with this woman. And now here she is trapping him with a baby and making sure he had no happiness with me. She dangled their daughter over his head which made him only to recent me. After we'd broken up, I'd noticed it was hard to contact Brock. I couldn't get him to reply to my text messages, phone call or anything else like I'd used to whenever we got into a disagreement. Maybe he was done this time, besides he'd only had a few more weeks before Noel was here. That's the name he'd picked out for the baby. I just wanted to know if everything was okay.

After trying and trying to get in contact with him, I finally got my answer. It was the 4th of July weekend. I'd been drinking and I wanted to know why I hadn't heard from Brock. I called him like crazy this day until he finally picked up. He told me that he was working on things with his family and he was sorry. That he didn't know how to tell me. He was heartbroken because he didn't wanna be without his daughter. He said he didn't answer because he was always with his baby momma and she was always around because she breastfed their baby. Before he could finish I burst into tears; drunken tears. The tears that already knew the answer, but only hurt to hear. The kind of tears where it felt like I was being shot and the only way to let some type of pain out was to cry. I cried so hard that my heart literally felt like it was breaking. He'd apologized over and over. He assured me to stop crying and that I would be okay. He chuckled a bit after my screaming and angry words I let fly off my tongue. I hated and loved him at the same time. I wanted him to hurt like I did. But I knew I couldn't. And she? I'm sure she was happy. She's got what she wanted. Her family, her 'husband' and no one could stand in the way of that now that she had that baby.

From that day on Brock and I never talked again. He'd seem like he'd got all he wanted. Everything he's ever said to me was a lie, and it sucked that it took a woman to trap him and hurt me in the process to see his true colors. What was I supposed to do? It felt hard to go on. All my friends felt so bad for me, they tried to comfort me the best way they could. But there was no use. I was heartbroken, I felt stupid. I mean what was I supposed to expect? This taught me a valuable lesson. About girlfriends, men who aren't really single, history with people, and most of all? Men. I had lost my best friend and someone I thought I loved all within the same time frame. Instead of letting this hurt me I let it motivate me. I try to take things slower and not act off of emotions. I'm an adult right? We all walk around here like we've got it all figured out. As an adult

you wanna believe that you have everything figured out.

But as a woman? We think everything is a sign, especially

when it comes to love.

WET WRITING

By: Cheraee C.

Rose red was his favorite hue so Lira preordered the sexiest and skimpiest piece of lingerie she could find online. She hid it under a peacoat precisely. She had some magnified, licentious motives and planned to entice her fiancé Leven with her exterior, and then entice him with her interior. However, he wanted to endow his infatuation was fine with her.

On the rooftop of her loft building, it was a candlelight feast waiting for them. Leven only had an appetite for Lira's body and she was even more appetizing when she let her peacoat hit the ground. You could tell by the luscious smile on his smooth, chocolate face they was about to ignite some April fireworks in a New York minute.

After Leven hugged her tightly and let his hands explore her petite, chocolate curves, he stripped down to nothing, but ripped, tattooed skin. Lira's one of a kind sultry garment was ready to surrender her bare skin, but only at Leven's leisure.

Lifting Lira up in the air like a castle, he sat her down on the edge of the rooftop. It sounds scary, being so close to the edge of life, but it wasn't. Feeling outer body adrenaline rushes, as the two kissed Leven lifted up Lira's negligee and began stimulating her juicebox with a sporadic, finger rotation. She became wetter instantly because her thoughts and her desires already had her mentally wet.

"It's been 3.5 years and a month since we had sex," Leven stated.

"Technically you can't count the first time baby, it was just a test-run. My memory is a little fuzzy though; why don't you get ready to twiddle me with your fiddle,"

"I been reminiscing about this very day Lira, I just hope you do more squirting then you do running."

"I've been saving myself for you as well. Pleasure is pain so I'm gonna take every inch of you even if I gotta scream, scratch, shake, bite, squeeze, clinch, or pinch.

Leven teased Lira's clit with his joystick, and in the same instance he used his free hand to caress and fondle her breasts. Lira had never seen Leven's penis before, but now that she was feeling it swipe back and forth between her legs, she knew for a fact it was long, thick, and fat. She thought to herself,

"Damn, I can't wait to feel him deep inside of me. This is going to be by far the greatest sex I ever had, and he had too."

She rubbed his hand across his chiseled chest using her fingers to outline his packs. A second later, she threw her head back and arched her back as he entered her foreign origins. In the same motion, he took a free hand and be stroked her with finesse up, down, left, right, side to side, hard, long, deep and repeatedly as her juices leaked and seeped off of her legs and onto the concrete. He pulled her

hair, he put his fingers in her mouth and let her taste her

vagina as he pounded her in every dimensional position he

could think of. Lira moaned and screamed so blissfully, it

was too much space for her voice to echo through the

noiseless air. They made love repeatedly until the both of

them collapsed on the red carpet she had spread out under

the table, and cuddled up with her peacoat. That was just

enough heat for them for comfort with the warm, humid

April breezes blowing and flowing by.

Love you baby, I wish upon a star that vision was

real. Lira ended her letter drawing a

kissy emoji next to her signature. She folded it two times so

it would have two neat creases and stuck it into a standard

sized white envelope. She wished she could seal her erotic

fantasy with some red lipstick. Unless she wanted her wet

letter rejected and returned, she had better stick to a lick of

saliva because lipstick and perfume wasn't allowed on

inmate mail. Finally Leven was goin get his snippet of what making love to Lira would be like. Lira was a writer and Leven had read many of Lira's hit, sex scenes. Now he finally had his very own sex scene to add to his mail collection. Lira had Sage's inmate address memorized so she wrote their two addresses in cursive letters and reached in her wallet for a stamp. She peeled the stamp off and pressed it onto the corner of the envelope. Grabbing her envelope, she walked out the door and headed to the post office. In a couple of business days, Leven was going to get a reminiscent letter he would keep secured under his mattress in his cell, and read again and again until he was freed.

Blurred Connotation

From her poetic love story "Conflicts of My Mind and Heart"

Written By: Sunshine Sims

I'm looking deep into their eyes hoping they can see

See all the feelings I feel for them even though it may seem unreal

As unreal to them as having to leave and start over is going to be

Turning over every rock, but caressing every part

Ignoring phone calls, but sending instant messages over the telephone watts

I'm not a little girl, you're not a little boy, but we both have kids that play with toys

And mates that feels their emotions are being played with liked toys

But I want to hold you, that's what you say

I tell you I want to see you and need you in every way

You don't want to be needed, you've been needed all your life

But I'm sorry you've met a married woman, who now is contemplating being your wife

Where is that line between, Love and Hate, as a matter of fact they said it's thin

Just like the movie "They Live" when you put on the glasses you truly see what's within

I , I, I, I , I , I I, I, I, I ,I ,I ,I ,I ,I WANT You is all I can say

And this is said both ways even though my eyes keep saying I LOVE YOU EVERDAY

Plenty Temptation

From her poetic love story "Conflicts of My Mind and Heart"

Written By: Sunshine Sims

You hear the songs on the radio?

Talking about that love you oh so want, but you left because you claim you're not ready though.

You go online and see their face, as you look around all alone in your new place.

See this is why you need them; this is why you want them; you remember what it's like to be in their presence

 But in essence, truth be told you want them more than you know, you've already cross those lines

They're flooding your dreams, thoughts and constantly on the mind

You've allowed your desire to give birth to sin

You've allowed your eyes to look within

You've allowed your heart to play the violin

You've put your mind on a spin, thrown in the wind

Walking in deep thought lost in steamy intentions

In the valley of love rain deep emotions

Dreaming, wishing and hoping to smell their air

Now all you tell yourself is it's not fair…

Finnessin'

By: J Focuz

He stood there and listened to the rain as it hit the top of the cars parked in the lot of the theater as he waited patiently for Christina to arrive. She wasn't typically late when they went out, but being the third date there was really no telling. Darryl hadn't been on many dates and it just so happens he bagged Christina who was completely out of his league and he knew it. His timing couldn't be better as he looked down at his phone and a text had come through. It was a text from Christina.

"Sorry I'm a little late," the message read.

"I'll be pulling up shortly."

That sounds like good news. Darryl goes in to purchase the romantic comedy the critics have been raving about online. "Fools in Love is comedic genius filled with romance, death, and passion," read one of the reviews. Had to be a snoozer let Darryl tell it but she was thrilled about him asking her to see it.

She arrived about ten minutes after the text and had looked as gorgeous as ever. Natural, curly hair was Darryl's thing. Besides the curves above her chin that mattered most, her body was banging and every time they went out she turned heads. "You ready?"

"Yeah, hey. Sorry I got a little busy today but I'm here," Christina replied. She wore this dress, much too nice for the movies but perfect for dinner that hugged each and every curve. The smell of popcorn flooded the sense as they gave their tickets to the ticket taker. She grabbed his arm and pointed like a kid in a candy store. Just after three dates, which mind you were the only times they've hung out, this fool was pretty much sprung.

After a movie, large popcorn, drinks and a long island for the lady, the date so far was at $48.15. Everywhere they went it seemed like he spent large amounts of money and it began to become a pattern to Darryl, but not just yet. He figured they were both having fun and spending time together, plus she was a catch, so it was worth it. He actually managed to stay awake through the movie and decided it was actually pretty good. That's the moment she got hungry.

"That movie was great. Especially the ending oh my God, I almost cried," said Christina.

"Adding up my account that makes two of us," thought Darryl.

"I'm starving," said Christina.

"Yeah, honestly I could eat," said Darryl.

They decided to meet at J. Alexander's on 8 Mile and Haggerty. It was a fancy steak joint that Darryl had never been to. They separated to their individual cars and met there. The place was busy as hell with what looked like absolutely no seating. After driving around the lot a few times and finally spotting someone leaving a spot close to the door they parked. When they walked in no one was waiting and they were immediately seated, much to Darryl's surprise. The room smelled mostly of steak and onions and being seated near the bar, the barley of the beer being served had also made its arrival to the senses. The table had several candles lit for added ambiance effect. Darryl had to admit the place was nice, a little too nice.

She ordered the surf and turf and he just went with a steak, butterfly medium well. Before either of the two could finish, the waitress brought the bill. It was $62.36. After drinks, it had most certainly become an expensive night at $110.51. The third in a row. He wiped his mouth with the cloth and pulled out his phone. It had seemed like during the meal she had constantly been on hers so he decided to check her Snapchat. He had just made one the previous day and it had recommended her as a friend. However, he hadn't added her yet.

The first picture he saw was a picture of her ticket stub for the movie. The caption read "Got bored so I stepped out. Fools In Love was AMAZING."

"Hmmm," thought Darryl. "No mention of me." He moved to the next photo and it was the straw that had broken the camel's back. She had taken a picture of her plate, alone, with a caption reading "Sometime you have to treat yourself."

"Hey sweetie, can you give me a second I gotta use the bathroom right quick." said Darryl.

"No problem," replied Christina with her head in her phone as it buzzed into the night. So much so, she didn't notice him quickly slip out the door snagging a toothpick on the way out.

"THE WORRIES OF A DREAMER"

By: Lawrence J.

Maybe I'm chasing the wrong dream,

maybe my window of opportunity has passed.

Maybe I'm too old to become what I'm pursing,

maybe I was meant to wallow in self-doubt

or maybe I'm letting fear control my destiny instead of me.

Maybe no one knows the answer to these questions but me.

Maybe a life without trying to pursue my dreams

no matter how big or small would haunt me.

Maybe if I just pushed a little harder I will become greater.

Maybe if I gave a little less time to worry, fear, self doubt,

pity, social media and focusing on cuffing season I will be great.

Maybe...I just need a drink.

Maybe if I replaced "maybe"

with phrases like. "I am unstoppable", "don't take no for answer," "today is the day you win" or began the day with a pray to the Lord

or whatever self affirmation I'll like best.

I wouldn't be watching success I'd be there.

"THE WAY SHE SAYS MY NAME"

By: Lawrence J.

1.Lust

Damn I hate that word LUST. WHAT DOES IT MEAN...?
I think I know the L is 4 looking from a far yeah that's it.
The U is 4 the urge yeah...yeah that's it. The S is 4 the
sexual tension I feel when ur around ME or WHEN I
HEAR UR NAME. And the T is 4 the way I wanna
TOUCH U and also the THINGS WE WILL DO WHEN U
READ THIS NOTE. Oh well that's just me what do u think
it means?

2. Would U Mine

play Janet Jackson's WOULD U MINE.....I said baby just
stop playin and come over here she said no I wanna make u
want ME EVEN more okay DADDY. She started on my
neck and gives a kiss then she licked me from my neck to
my balls. Soon after dat I was handcuffed and eatin her
out...yeah I do it so what. Baby girl was shakin like never
before and dropped it back on me like never before don't
forget I'm blindfolded and handcuffed but she starts to
scream so I had to.......go even harder but soon after she
started to scream SHE HAD TO WAKE UP....WET AS
HELL AND PISSED OFF. AND CALLIN ME ON DA
PHONE TELLIN ME ALL ABOUT IT.

3. SEX

What is it she asked me my dick I said damn baby....is what
she said. what I said you surprised? yeah baby you grew up
since middle school...I guess so is what I said. damn BIG
DADDY is what she said next. then as she grabbed me she

gasped and let me in and said do you LOVE ME I said yeah she said now let me ride. THEN after it was over I asked what is SEX? She said LET ME SHOW YOU BIG...AND I DO MEAN BIG DADDY.

4. THE way she says my name it just makes me wanna fuck her for DAYZ. awww THE way she does what she do to me makes me wanna say DAMN I LOVE U GURL. the way she TOUCHES me leads 2 the way she KISSES me and that leads 2 the way she scratches me and oooo that leads 2 the way she says my name softly but loudly hen...hen....HENRY! DONT STOP PLEASE DONT STOP! FASTER Oooo.... that's the spot daddy rite there then she screams aww FUCK ME BABY...aww this DICK IS GOOD BABY GIVE 2 ME BABY please. and then she scratches my back while pulling me closer and say ever so gently almost in a whisper HeNRY...

5. I HATE BITCH ASS NIGGAS
Why? because he took her away from me cuz he thinks I'm fucking her. BITCH ASS daddy of hers he don't even give a fuck about my BABY. it's funny as hell cuz he tryna stop us but he don't know what we do. I'm TELL him he got da game fucked up. why? cuz my baby love me.....and I laugh every time he try break us up...HE JUST don't know I'm her DADDY.... HA HA now go get bent BITCH.

"SOMETIMES"

By: PDot

Sometimes I got Hate on my back,

sometimes I wish that I can rewind the time to about 10

years back.

Sometimes I smoke blunts of the loud, no matter how much

I take and blow,

the problems staying around.

Sometimes I know that I should humble and pray,

sometimes I wonder why things just don't go away.

Sometimes I know I deal with shit every day,

I could just take the easy way out... just pick up and spray.

A wise once told me... see if you're gonna do dirt...

you better do it by your lonely.

Sometimes I feel the world be hoe-ing me,

I call myself RESPECT you only get me if you earn me.

The world? I treat it like an avenue

It'll come to an end, and if the Lord sees fit..

Hell let me live again.

But sometimes… I think my foes is cooler than my kin,

and that's when reality set in.

Sometimes…

What's up with the stereotype?

I'm not your typical broad,

I'm the type that ride-or-die for my negus who call

Sometimes I feel like…

Is this shit worth going through it all?

With all the cake ass niggas trying to poison my walls?

Sometimes I wish I never ran into the men that I did,

don't wanna take care of they own, but claim another

bitches' kids?

But then again I'm sort of glad I did,

cause now I peep a niggas game before he even part his

lips.

It used to be… I like? I let you hit,

now put them benji's on the table before I even part my

hips.

Used to be treated like an adolescent chick,

now I don't care what YOU got because I got my own grip.

You walking?... Me? I got my own whip.

Sometimes I'm on that other shit and treat a nigga like a

trick.

Sometimes... I feel like I'm taken for a ride,

when it's all over with...

I'll meet you on the other side... SOMETIMES!

"INEXPLICIT"

By: Cheraee C.

I'm so inexplicit, I didn't use to be

sometimes I miss it

a few exes are idealistic

who would kill to kiss it?

would purchase first class Delta tickets to kick it

the desire and admire thickens

the celibacy and marriage crickets

try to discourage me so discouragingly

I'm a temple with a template of exquisiteness

I can't give free snippets, previews, or peeks

Its a certain type of intimacy I want

I'm over the skepticism of typical intimacy as much as I

want intimacy

I remain inexplicit

I've seen addiction in so many addictive souls

my threshold represents goals, values, and codes

I treat my gifts like platinum jewels of silver and gold

I want to elope and float into the inter scope of pure

romance,

but romance is so remote I don't feel a connection to

romance

I don't think romance will chance me because it never has

it's like a passageway I will never pass

I mine as well quit and go back to being explicit

cuz don't no happiness got my name on it

except a single one that's singular

I'll never jump the broom and have a foreign honeymoon

I can't even get a Valentine let alone a date

all I get is strictly explicit vibes from secular guys with

worldly minds

I feel like my inexplicit attitude is gonna age

I'll be inexplicit forever and a day....

INFAMOUS

By: Cheraee C.

my smile spreads across my face like dimples

thoughts are ample between my trembles and temples

love is so occidental with a shooting star momentum

your mileage is far from my mileage like Sacramento

your infamous credentials give me a road running conquest

freeway and speedway ventures

going east and west

you use to be thee America's most wanted type

but, new leafs and loose-leaf, sentences and beliefs

got you a new verdict, a new image

no gimmicks, raw footage

I know hundreds who've crossed the same probate borders

and quarters

no more lawyers and disorder

sometimes it feels like you Afghanistan far

loving you is like a freestyle with 16 bars

not a day goes by

I'm thoughtless or speechless

I would never bark up a tree with no greenness

despite the infamous reputation you carry

I'm infatuated and captivated by the love you vary and

variations of it

it's level-less and levelness

like a concealed creation

everything that's infamous is bottomless and topless

no need for innovations

I love you exactly the way you are

you're infamously an inspiration....

"BREAKING POINT"

by: Cheraee C.

fateful, resentful, and vengeful

small talk you babble stalling

you fester and gesture enough

liquid courage pressure calling

whether I answer or your try goes unanswered

we're divided, but you resist falling

into the realm and slow jams of another woman

can you casually find you another causality?

gradually tryna ease back

dispassionately you lean back

actively you feign black

dreaming big dreams with a cracked screen

the facts are bare and unfair

you're deflated like four flats with no air

tryna serenade me with tarnished jewels

I never babysit my phone for you

I don't delicate my voice for you

I delegate free range and the shots I fire

you think I'm resentful and vengeful

if only I was a capsule

resentful, trapped soul

umindful, where's a blindfold?

I don't wanna see you

I don't even wanna reference you

why do we gotta have conversation?

my lack of communication

boosts your confidence, moves your ego

you wish you could boast about me

beyond your compliments and your invitations

I hit my breaking point with you a long time ago

don't expect any modifications....

VICTIM WHO?

By: Cheraee C.

lying lies and selling dreams

when the dream seeking becomes an era and a fatality

cold realities and technicalities

I'm morally resistant

rebuttals strike immoral puddles

the fingers are pointed

subliminally they are jointed and pointed

the cover-ups a cover story uncovered

the pastures in my heart remain undiscovered and

unpublished

the vows I want remain unaccomplished and unrelated

because your grade of love is sluggish

and I got the title I got

I'm supposed to be elated?

I'm in a big flux feeling underrated, basic, and civic

I'm too coloristic for this dullness

I just want the wholesome wholeness

the unbalance and hindrance

bass changes, word changes, communiqué changes

the narration I get from certain disparities and

dissimilarities

I can't classify where's the sullenness coming from?

why everybody want to be so hurt?

I'm the one that's reserved and curved

I never cry victim as many victims as I been

I'm so disclosed can't no disclosure bring the things

I have within me to a surface

I just want to live and give my purpose

all I did, all I do

 is specify my emotions

emotions I need to treat like symptoms

good try, but you ain't the victim

Excerpts from

Cheraee C. books

Deviancy: I Love The Thrill

Liq-Trocity

Another Shady Mission

On Another Shady Mission

The Shadiest Mission Ever

DEVIANCY
I Love The Thrill

BY CHERAEE C.

DEVIANCY

Introduction: The Art of Deviancy

The bureaucracy of Oakland law was flooded with a bunch of snooty, tight-creased suit wearing capitalists who were sexually oppressive with fetishes dying to be eased, challenged, and released. They used their downtime to prey on inner city sexually deviant citizens whom they could exploit with their government salary. No matter what city, state, or country you went to there was always a sex scandal somewhere. The queen of sex scandals in the hood though was a top flight erotic mogul who went by the name of Infiniti Brooks.

Infiniti Brook's raw reputation was so viral that she had enough colorful subscribers to start her own minority. From owning her own chain of adult stores (Infiniti SX), adult entertainment safe house, and owning her own sex toy line, Infiniti had all types of billionaires in her back pocket, fifth pocket, purse pocket, corner pocket, all pockets. Her billionaires couldn't stop mentally churning the motions that she would whip on them.

Lingering inside Infiniti's Lathrup Village branch was a local news anchor from Channel 4 (Quad Lewinski.) Quad was always the first to test Infiniti's sex toys. Her latest invention was known as "Pinnacle" and its sole purpose was to tantalize the vagina with an array of temperature changes. Quad wired Infiniti 1500 bucks every time he paid her a visit when she dropped a new toy. All Infiniti had to do was do a personal demonstration for Quad as he sat back, loosened up his tie, let his dress pants drape on his ankles, fondled himself, and watched. Infiniti and Quad was making way to their usual dressing room after Infiniti grabbed a Pinnacle off the shelf, but Quad stopped her dead in her tracks.

78

"Infiniti, have you checked your account?"

"No, I didn't. You ain't never played me on my monies before. Should I?"

"I put 3000 in your account today. I know we've had a mean streak and I ain't trying to break it, but today I want to watch a new gal play with herself. Is that cool?"

"That's cool with me; I gotta shoot some moves anyway. Let me go holler at my girl Navy. You can just wait in the room back there and I'll send her in. I'll give her the toy too. No need for my use."

"Cool."

Good, I didn't feel like playing with myself anyway. I'm a C.E.O. what I look like? Maybe Quad and I should negotiate another deal. I'll give him a new girl every time he comes to play, and I'll switch up the branches too long as he pays what he weighs. I still don't understand why he won't let me setup these personal sessions at a hotel or something, but that's another topic for another day. Hopefully Navy will get down with the get down.

"Aye Navy, I need you to do something for me."

"Sure, what you need?"

"I have a client in the room who wants you to test out Pinnacle for him. Is you cool with that or nah?"

"I don't recall seeing masturbation in the job description."

"You wanna lose your promotion and raise all in a minute or do you won't this fat $500 dollar tip?"

"I'm tripping, which room he in?"

"He's in the last room to the left. All you got to do is test the toy out on yourself. He's not going to touch or nothing. All he wants to do is watch you. I'll transfer the $500 into your account before I leave. I gotta make a run. I don't know if I'll be back today so you know what to do. Here take the toy," Infiniti handed Navy the unopened box.

"You're not sending me in there with a creep are you or to be raped because if you are you can take this job and your $500 tip and shove it up your anus with a dry, plastic dildo."

"I told you I have high paying clients who pay me money to make their fantasies come true. I can put you on or put you out because you're stalling and your insulting my intelligence."

"I'm sorry I just never did anything so random like this before."

"It's a first time for everything. Think about the $500 and how much more money you can make especially if he requests you. This was all at his request. Now gone in there and get it over with before you scare him away."

Going in the room and closing the sound proof door behind her, Navy was more nervous than a student on the first day of school. She saw Quad sitting across from her waiting for the show to begin. Navy closed her eyes and took a deep breath. She was just about to unbutton her skinny jeans when Quad broke her concentration.

"Your nametag says Navy is that how you pronunciate it?"

"Yeah you said it right."

"I rocks with Infiniti the long way, but I need a new deviant girl. Do you think you can handle that role?"

"I'm scoring roles and never once thought about acting or the big screen," Navy thought.

Quad went in his pockets and pulled out a wad of money. The wad held ten 100 dollar bills tightly.

"Here's 1000, watching is getting corny. That's what I paid Infiniti to do, but you I want you to test Pinnacle out on me. I'm Infiniti's product test dummy."

"Um, I don't think that's a good idea," Navy felt gauche.

"I'm not paying you to think or like my ideas."

"You are a male; you should use a male sex toy. Infiniti manufactured this toy for a female and the female anatomy. Unless you got a clitoris down there, this toy ain't for your alley."

"I do have a clitoris."

"How I thought you was a him? You mean to tell me you're really a shim? A she-he? A shemale?"

"Yeah I am now that you know let's get it cracking with Pinnacle. I got to hit the streets and follow up on some news leads."

"We ain't about to get nothing cracking. Only thing you need to crack is some Chap Stick for your dry, crusty lips. I feel like I just got catfished so here's what's about to happen. I'm going to keep your generous tip and forget this ever happened. We'll let Infiniti think what she thinks, and next time you return you'll be better off sticking with Infiniti. If you got a problem with this arrangement I can go to your job and tell them how you're lying about your gender and soliciting women for sex at local adult stores."

"Okay Navy, you pulled a fast one on me, I see the lesbianness all up in and through your corneas. This was just a warm-up, next time you'll fold. I'll catch you next time I'm jones'n if you're still employed here that is. Unless you're going to explain all of this to Infiniti, she's going to stick you and me in this same ole room again. So jokes on you baby girl, you have a nice day," Quadette left the room confident and cocky. She was going to get her monies worth one way or another. Now that she had the honors of turning a straight girl inside out, Navy was gonna reap what she just sowed. After five minutes of standing in the toy room, Navy peered around the shelves and corners. She didn't see Quadette in sight nor Infiniti, and she was the only employee on staff. She grabbed the mic off the counter and spoke through the store's intercom system.

"Attention all customers, there's an emergency so Infinity SX will be closing in five minutes please make your final selections and come to the register with your final purchases." Once the last customer checked out, Navy shut down the store, locked up, left the store key in the drop box, took her $1500 dollars, and quit. She hurried up and went to withdraw the $500 from her account before Infiniti could get whiff of her instant resignation. The art of sexual deviancy was not her cup of tea; she was going to leave that up to Infiniti. Infiniti never saw Navy again or Quad. Infiniti's employee turnover was sparse and Navy was the first employee in her chain of stores to ever quit. Still a funny story Infiniti often replayed in her head whenever new employees or new customers entered into her business.

LIQ-TROCITY

BY CHERAEE C.

LIQ-TROCITY

When shit got real...

"My brain is hanging upside down," was the daily aftermath of Chisel Simmons after his coast-to- coast pro basketball career became obsolete. No matter what he did to guarantee his success, his focus was remotely off, and he couldn't think logically without being easily side-tracked.

Chisel was a proficient, 10-year-Euroleague power forward who wore his number 7 jersey pompously. Everything changed when his physical aptitude shifted from athletic to un-athletic in a matter of seconds ending a fourth quarter.

Playing basketball overseas was the most optimistic decision that Chisel ever made for his basketball profession and everything was smooth at first, but life always finds an unyielding way to intervene. Oversea basketball players got paid less then what U.S. basketball players did, but they were spoiled with lots of amenities. They were given houses, cars, women, endorsements, clothing, more women, and anything they could ever envision. Chisel didn't have to spend a dime of his earnings, because he was worshipped by the sport, and the sport provided him with an affluent lifestyle he couldn't decline.

Just as Chisel was bypassing opponents, dribbling and crossing through the frontcourt, and scored the winning shot in his championship game; a game where his team excelled with a 111-78 blowout, something below his waist popped. Something felt looser than it ever felt before. Chisel's body buckled down on the court and the basketball went rolling to the stands. Chisel was in excruciating pain when paramedics were called to his aching rescue. After numerous imaging tests, an MRI, and annoying ass doctors, Chisel found out that he tore his ACL (anterior cruciate ligament) which was both a common and uncommon injury for a typical basketball

After being told that he would never be able to play basketball again on so many rehab and surgical occasions, Chisel knew damn well his career was over and preferred to embark on another career pathway because there was no way in hell he was going to risk injuring himself so traumatically again. Surgeries, rehabs, and doctors just weren't his thing, not to mention all the pain that he had to endure suffering, recuperating, and healing from his injury was unforgettable. Using crunches, limited physical activity, and wearing a leg brace wasn't his style either so Chisel began to self-medicate himself with alcohol. This loathsome period in his life became the beginning of a habit and future habits that he was never going to be able to shake out of his re-structured system.

Chisel's liquid demons made him become verbally abusive towards women, insecure, paranoid, sleep deprived, develop trust issues, act very irrationally and idiotically in the public eye, unsympathetic, and feel invalid. His liquid demons pretty much turned him into an unrecognizable monster at intoxicating levels.

Chisel had a house so grandiose that it should've been featured on MTV Crib's for all of its perks and was just all-around grandeur. Chisel was a definite father of two sons and two possible daughters. He was a ladies' man who changed women like he changed draws, with a wife still hanging on the back-burner. One day he planned to divorce his first and current wife, Haze Hilton, when he felt like Fed-Exing her ass back to Korea. Until then, he was just going to have to deal with her wifely bullshit, but since they were separated and she was a hooker, her wifely bullshit was only going to get worst.

Years later, Chi   ney flow was like a car dealership full of armored money trucks loaded with stacks and racks of money. Chisel could do whatever the hell he wanted to do in his liquid life and nobody could stop him. From time to time, Chisel still made money off of his retired talent by doing interviews, hosting basketball events, hosting parties, private appearances, endorsements, and etc so he was never money-hungry.

The sad part about Chisel and his love life was that he put too much emphasis in color complexity in correlation with the women he chose to be with. He had a light skin and white skins is the right skin complex so he never found himself dating, fucking, or even eye-fucking a caramel skinned or dark skinned woman because his skin complex was high and mighty. Chisel was definitely selling himself short, but as far as Chisel knew he knew everything, his preference was his preference, and nobody could tell him any different.

The light skinned and white skinned women he loved really loved him. They were never in love with him for the money, but he was too lost in addiction to grasp the true concept of love so he let his liquid dependence drive his women insane. As far as he was concerned no woman would ever be able to make him conquer his liquid fetishes not even his wife, not his daughter if and when he had one that wasn't in question, not a trick, not a side-bitch, and not even his own mother. Chisel was going to be an alcoholic until he drunk himself into a coma and died unless life decided differently.

In the meantime in between time Chisel had better get his shattered life together before his life was like paper shreds in a paper shredder because Chisel was going to have a rude awakening and it wasn't going to be enough fire extinguishers to sav   e from burning into flames.

ANOTHER SHADY MISSION

ANOTHER SHADY MISSION

BY CHERAEE C.

ANOTHER SHADY MISSION

Introduction

Every saint has a past, and every sinner has a future, but for Passive Boone Mitchell and Darnell "Smoke" Mitchell everything they had and would have was a catch 22. The prominent areas in the city of Detroit were their paradise, but the dubious snakes of Detroit were their hell. The dynamic couple was still in the newlywed stages of their courthouse marriage, but nothing not even eternity was ever going to snatch them apart. Even though Passive wanted to be the first family member in her Boone family to have a real wedding, she refused to have a real wedding without her father. Every father may dread the day they have to walk their daughter down the aisle and put their daughter's life and heart in the hands of a man, but still every father is there for that moment, but Passive was denied that chance. So for Passive, she was more in love with her ring and her husband then submitting to society's typical wedding norms.

Passive who was thirty-six college credits away from being a licensed social worker, put her dream on hold for her wifely transporter duties. Smoke who was a very compassionate man, wanted to run for mayor of his city, because he had some revenge he was dying to serve cold on behalf of Passive and his deceased father-in-law. Passive's father Syrian Boone was head of security for the current mayor of Detroit, who was Mayor Cahill Caesar. Cahill and Syrian were childhood best friends, but once their friendship was tested Cahill buckled. One late working night, Syrian entered Cahill's office to do his regular check, and make sure Cahill was still breathing, and the surroundings weren't breached. When Syrian walked in on Cahill, Cahill was committing infidelity with a King of Diamond's stripper all the top executive men in the D knew as Basil. Syrian practically had a heart attack because Cahill was Syrian's brother-in-law which meant Cahill was cheating on Syrian's sister. Instead of having a heart attack, Syrian snatched Basil off of Cahill's half-naked body and yanked her into the nearest bookshelf, and beat Cahill until he was unrecognizable. Of course Cahill wasn't going to let Syrian get away with beating up the no good mayor so Cahill had Syrian arrested for every charge that the city should've been bringing upon Cahill himself. In rebuttal, Syrian encouraged Cahill to drop all of his pending charges, or he was going to tell his beloved sister about Cahill's faithlessness, and he was going to be the cause of the biggest publicity and scandals surrounding a mayor in history. Cahill thought Syrian was just bluffing, until

Syrian started meeting with local news reporters, radio stations, and local magazine editors. Syrian even got a tape recording from Basil with her admitting that she had an affair with the mayor, and she knew three other women who were having an affair with the mayor as well. Once the naked truth began leaking out like water from a leaking pipe, in Cahill's eyes death was the only penalty. A couple days before their trial begun, Cahill had Syrian murdered in prison in his defenseless sleep. At this time, Smoke had just popped the big question to Passive, and Passive couldn't wait to tell her father, and show him her immaculate ring. She always visited him as much as she could, and her father had shared with her everything he possibly could about Mayor Cahill because he knew his days were numbered. Passive was the main plug to Syrian leaking out all of Mayor Cahill's dirty deeds so she knew everything. The only thing she didn't know was that her father was dead until her last visit went unvisited, and instead of sitting behind a 2-way window gazing into her father's green eyes, she began the grieving process as she found out her father was dead. When those words were murmured to her, she knew exactly who did it and why, and she knew that she wasn't going to die without making sure Mayor Cahill and his affiliates felt her wrath.

Passive's support for her husband was limitless. And she was willing to take all or nothing risks just so that they could make everyone responsible for her father's death go straight to hell.

They did practically everything together, and by Smoke becoming a cop, there was a lot of more riskier things they were going to be doing together. During Smoke's first days of being an official cop, there was a lot of talk throughout the precinct about people stealing drugs out of the evidence room. Every single one of those cops got caught, because they weren't smart enough, they weren't fast enough, and they weren't grimy enough, but not Smoke. He had all the qualifications and skills it took to be an inside man. After some soul-searching he decided he was going to steal a load of drugs every full moon, and began a drug enterprise of his own, and his wife was going to be the deliverer. This was a decision that him and Passive made together on behalf of their dreams. They had lots of real estate properties all over the United States, they had lots of connections, they had the perfect motives, they had lots of stamina, and mostly they had each other. As unstable as they seemed, the past had a cold reality for them that was more   vastating than the future.

BASED ON A TRUE STORY

ON ANOTHER SHADY MISSION

BY CHERAEE C.

Prologue

Nobody adapts the psychology of killing overnight and for Passive the trigger she clutched that killed her ex-drug connect Champagne wasn't the first. Her past may have seemed like it was inerrant, but it wasn't. Passive had more skeletons in her closet then a haunted mansion.

The day when Passive's mugshot met the 11th precinct's booking department and Smoke was substituting for a booking officer was the historical, unthinkable day that the ultimate couple met. Smoke actually took two enthralling mugshots and fingerprints of Passive and she had the sexiest mugshot that he had ever seen. It was just everything about her that made him marvel at her unparalleled individuality.

"Passive Boone, I see you don't have any type of criminal history at all so why would you falsify your identification to a police officer?" Smoke questioned his arrestee like she was going to give him a straight answer.

"Technically I didn't falsify my identification. My nickname is Diamond so when the officer asked me for my name I said my name was Diamond. And by a glance on your badge your nickname is Smoke. I'm sure the name Smoke isn't printed anywhere on your birth certificate. I tried to explain this to the officer, but he insisted on arresting me."

"He probably just wanted to see your ass in handcuffs and be seen driving your fine ass around the city."

"If that's his idea of a fantasy then I guess."

"You must've not been staring in the mirror lately because we don't arrest women of your stature every day."

"And now you're flirting. Who flirts with a woman in handcuffs? Don't I seem suspect to you? You actually believe my explanation for this disarray?" Passive asked.

"I believe you and that's exactly why I'm going to go squash this with my officers right now."

"I'm not trying to bust your little dutiful bubble, but my daddy works for the mayor so don't get your little "officer" connects misconstrued with mines. I've never made it to a holding cell before, and trust me I'm not going to see one today. Just wait on it you'll see."

Ten minutes after Passive was brought into the 11th precinct mayor Cahill's lawyer Drew was barging in the precinct's doors to free her. When the arresting officer was sitting in his squad car running Passive's information, Passive took that small window to let her daddy know what was transpiring so he could tell Cahill and Cahill could take care of it. Although, Passive didn't have no right to be relying on Cahill after all the unknown lunacy she was stirring up in his organization, a plug was a plug. You get what you give, and since Cahill was giving out shade, Passive was giving shade back.

Speeding was the reason the officer stopped Passive in the mist of her early bird adrenaline rush. Passive was ghostly taking down Cahill's organization and was killing off his workers one by one, and had just successfully killed another disloyal employee which would make it her fifth slaying.

Mayor Cahill was supposed to be an honorable man and Passive's godfather, but what kind of godfather propositions his goddaughter for sex? What kind of godfather hires one of his workers to try to take his goddaughter's virginity? What kind of godfather is the number one suspect in your goddaughter's mother's unfortunate disappearance?

Of course Passive's father Syrian knew nothing about all these things that were manifesting behind his daughter's closed curtains. If he would've found out Cahill would've been ten feet under. Passive couldn't bear to be the reason why her father spent the rest of his life in the prison system so she kept his shadiness on the hush and found a silent way to deal with her definition of redemption. Since her daddy was a professional security guard, a gun instructor, a nightclub security manager to over five nightclub establishments in the D, a single father, plus plenty more job fortes, Syrian had to instill his security skills within his daughter.

Smoke was the only man that Passive had ever shared all of her innermost secrets with and that's exactly how they made it to become a ride or die couple. The day that finally shined light on the true Cahill was Passive's father's murder. She had always been contemplating the day that they would cross paths again. She knew it was going to be soon, she just didn't know when. All Passive knew was her crazy life created a street girl named Diamond who was not to be underestimated, underrated, or understated.

BASED ON A TRUE STORY

THE SHADIEST MISSION EVER

BY CHERAEE C.

THE SHADIEST MISSION EVER

Chapter 1: Shady Intent

Clinging onto her hospital gown like a souvenir, Omani refused to take the thin, cotton eyesore off.

"Omani please take that infirmary rag off. I can't be wandering around in public with you looking like a mental case."

"I don't want too; this gown is the closest emblem of motherhood I have left to Amory besides my cervical stitches so I'm not taking it off until we get her back," Omani proceeded to fold her arms together like a spoiled rich kid who's credit card got declined.

"I promise you we're going to get her back, but you got to lose the grandma suit. You look like an outcast right now. Nobody is going to take us criminally serious if we both aren't dressed to par."

Ready to transition from grieving mother to stone cold killer, Omani finally decided to ease out her hospital threads. It had been weeks since Omani wore real clothes. Since Omani and Onyx were on a mission, Onyx stepped out and chose some swanky pieces for his baby mother from her favorite boutique. Her spirits were lower than an old juke box trying to play a blues song. Her gloomy days were just temporary though because her and Onyx were about to impose their stratagem of retribution.

"I never wanted you to see my dark side Omani, but now the shit is inevitable."

"What are you talking about Onyx? Have you ever even owned a gun, loaded a gun or shot a gun before? I think not."

"You got jokes Omani. Let me tell you a little bit about my thuggish ruggish ways."

REWIND: Once upon a time, Onyx was an assembly line worker for the big 3 at the Ford Rouge Factory. He used to break niggas in the crannies of a warehouse for the owner of an automotive cartel whose name was Fess. Factory plants were colossal and earsplitting, and unless somebody pulled a fire alarm or spoke into an intercom, you wouldn't be able to hear a man cry for help even if he howled like a wolf.

Fess had economical ties with the big 3 and ties to the big 3's workers. Fess had at least a 1000 ways of getting money and two of those ways included pushing cocaine through the Ford plants and using company vehicles to push weight and company drivers. He proved that it was definitely some slick jokers in this world, and even though there was lots of money to be made and getting made in this organization, a thief was always being birthed every 60 seconds. After Fess saw Onyx put his paws on this worker Mitch, he knew off rip he wanted Onyx to be his hitta. Three perfect jabs and Onyx ended up putting Mitch in a coma. Mitch shouldn't have been lying on his baby dick and telling all the other workers at the plant he smashed Omani. At that time, nobody was smashing Omani except for Onyx. Onyx warned Mitch the first time he heard Mitch talking cash shit about how he was going to fuck Omani, how he knew Omani was digging him. Mitch didn't take heed to Onyx's forewarning though. Purposely, Mitch kept insulting and disrespecting Omani with his irritating and irrational ass insinuations. All Onyx wanted to do was his job, but Mitch made him snap like a camera. If he got fired, he got fired, so fucking be it. Onyx tried to ignore Mitch, but his ignorance was too flamboyant for that. Anybody who puts a co-worker in a coma should've been sued, fired, or facing criminal charges, but not Onyx. Fess was too impressed by Onyx's heavyweight skills that he had to promote Onyx to his team.

"So Onyx you know why you're in my office right? Fess cross-examined his new protégé.

"Y'all honestly can just fire me over the phone. I don't need no sit-down to get fired." Onyx stood up as if he said his peace ready to dip.

"I would never fire somebody with such lethal hands when I can utilize their services."

"What's the catch?"

"Long story short, I'm a business man and niggas love to get out of line with me. When they get out of line you ruff them up however you want too. I'll pay you five bands a thrashing. If you refuse my offer then you can consider yourself fired and remove your rambunctious ass from my premises."

Precisely, Onyx envisioned all the bands he could make just to KO a bunch of hand-picked, weak niggas every other blue moon and he was down for the challenge. It wasn't like he really had an affirmative choice anyways.

"I'm down," and just like that any nigga that fucked over Fess got served a knuckle sandwich by Onyx. Fucking with Onyx and his fists you either ended up in a coma, in ICU, or in a morgue. Everything was cool until Fess disappeared off the face of Detroit. With Onyx's reputation in mind he took this opportunity as a way to put his Ford days behind him and resign.

$

Little did Omani know that Amory was not Onyx's only child. Two years ago, when Omani and Onyx were on expendable terms, he fathered a daughter named Corrine by a woman named Cortina. His daughter Corrine had the exact, same birthday as his new daughter Amory. When Onyx was at the hospital with Omani, it took him everything in his power not to have an emotional breakdown over Corrine or new fatherhood.

When Corrine was born, Onyx was locked up in the pen upstate. Somehow Cortina got into some trouble with Child Protective Services and their daughter was put into foster care. Onyx called and called Cortina to find out exactly what the bitch had done, but Cortina never answered Onyx's calls. Whether Cortina had somebody else in the picture or not was none of Onyx's concern. He just wanted to make sure his baby girl was straight.

Since Onyx was incarcerated he couldn't save Corrine from the evil system so the state took it upon itself to terminate the rights of both parents all due to the severity of offenses against Cortina's and Onyx's inability to be active parents.

The only person besides the parents who knew about this secret child was Onyx's mother Oni, but since Onyx didn't have an ongoing son-mother type of bond with her his secret wasn't exposable. Onyx begged his mother Oni to take care of her granddaughter until he came home, but she refused. What type of grandmother would refuse to care for her only grandchild? Oni didn't have any reason to refuse caring for baby Corrine temporarily. No matter what pretenses stood against Corrine, Oni blatantly refused. She claimed she wanted nothing to do with Onyx, his life, or anybody in it. This situation is the reason why Onyx and Oni don't have and will never have a functional relationship. As far as he was concerned, he didn't have a mother, he raised himself.

When Onyx got released from jail from doing a bid on a probation violation, he tried to find Corrine, but she was lost in the system. It was like she had a new identity all of a suddenly. Besides, Onyx didn't have any legal rights to Corrine anymore so in court he didn't stand a chance. He didn't want too, but he had to let the memory of Corrine go. Hopefully, one day they would be reunited someway, somehow.

Now that he had baby Amory that was his second chance of true fatherhood. He was hoping this time nothing would go wrong, but it was too late for that because everything that could possibly be wrong was wrong. It was like Onyx wasn't meant to be a father because every baby he has had has experienced some type of adversity because they can't even reach the age of 1 without walking a thin line. Onyx better hope and pray that Omani never finds out about his other child, because if she does Onyx is probably going to be buried up under a viaduct somewhere. It didn't matter that this was a child that Onyx fathered while the two was on a break, it was the fact that Onyx felt comfortable and attached enough to let his sperm swim in another bitch's ovaries while the two was on a break is exactly how Omani was going to see it. It will be no coming back for Onyx so hopefully nobody ever leaks his secret.

$

PLAY: Now here Onyx was still riding with his black-hearted girl Omani about to take lives and kill things. They were two thoroughbred parents willing to abominate a whole planet for their precious pride and joy-Amory. Out of nowhere a sense of pleasure came over Onyx like a typical man. He began fondling her breasts, her nipples, and her areolas with his hands in a very teasing way. Then he lifted up her shirt and pulled her perky breasts out her bra one at a time trading attention from one to the other. Usually, Omani was never aroused by breast fondling and titty sucking, but today was different. As inconsolable as Omani was she couldn't help, but to throw her head back, arch her back, bite her lips a bit, moan, and tremble. Then Onyx took his fingers and began circling and twirling them on the outer origins of her vagina. Both of them were ready to knock each other off physically, but mentally Omani couldn't take it there so Omani pushed Onyx flat back into his seat.

"Chill Onyx I can't do this."

"Why not you know you want too?"

"Doesn't matter I just had a baby and our baby just got kidnapped. This isn't the time or the place for this."

"I think we should have sex before we go killing folks. Who knows this could be our last chance to have sex with each other. It's no telling what or where the road ahead is going to lead us to or through."

"In your mind you better scroll down memory lane of all the times we fucked because that's the best that I can do for you right now," and just like that the rapture was lost. It was time for them to settle some scores and for them to be the leaders of their amber alert. Amory Mitchell was coming home, Lindsay Chambers was going to die slowly, and both Onyx and Omani were going to see to it.

BOOK CATALOG

Available on Amazon, Amazon Kindle

Cheraeec.com and Mocypublishing.com